D0490772

My Mummy is
MAGIC

First published 2006 by Macmillan Children's Books

This edition published 2007 by Macmillan Children's Books
a division of Macmillan Publishers Ltd
20 New Wharf Road, London N1 9RR
Basingstoke and Oxford
Associated companies throughout the world
www.panmacmillan.com

ISBN: 978-1-4050-9023-0

Text copyright © Carl Norac 2006
Illustrations copyright © Ingrid Godon 2006

Moral rights asserted.

All rights reserved. No part of this publication may be reproduced, stored in or
introduced into a retrieval system, or transmitted in any form, or by any means (electronic,
mechanical, photocopying, recording or otherwise) without the prior written permission of
the publisher. Any person who does any unauthorised act in relation to this publication
may be liable to criminal prosecution and civil claims for damages.

1 3 5 7 9 8 6 4 2

A CIP catalogue record for this book
is available from the British Library.

Printed in Belgium by Proost

Carl Norac

My Mummy is
MAGIC

Illustrated by Ingrid Godon

MACMILLAN CHILDREN'S BOOKS

My mummy doesn't have
a pointy hat or a wand.
She doesn't need things
like that. My mummy
is magic anyway.

Sometimes I have nightmares, but my mummy chases the monsters away. That's magic.

If I whisper a secret in
my mummy's ear, she
guesses it before I've
finished telling her!
That's magic.

When I hurt myself,
my mummy kisses the
sore bit, and ta-da!
It's all better.
That's magic.

My favourite thing is
swimming with my mummy.
Together, we swim as fast
as a dolphin.

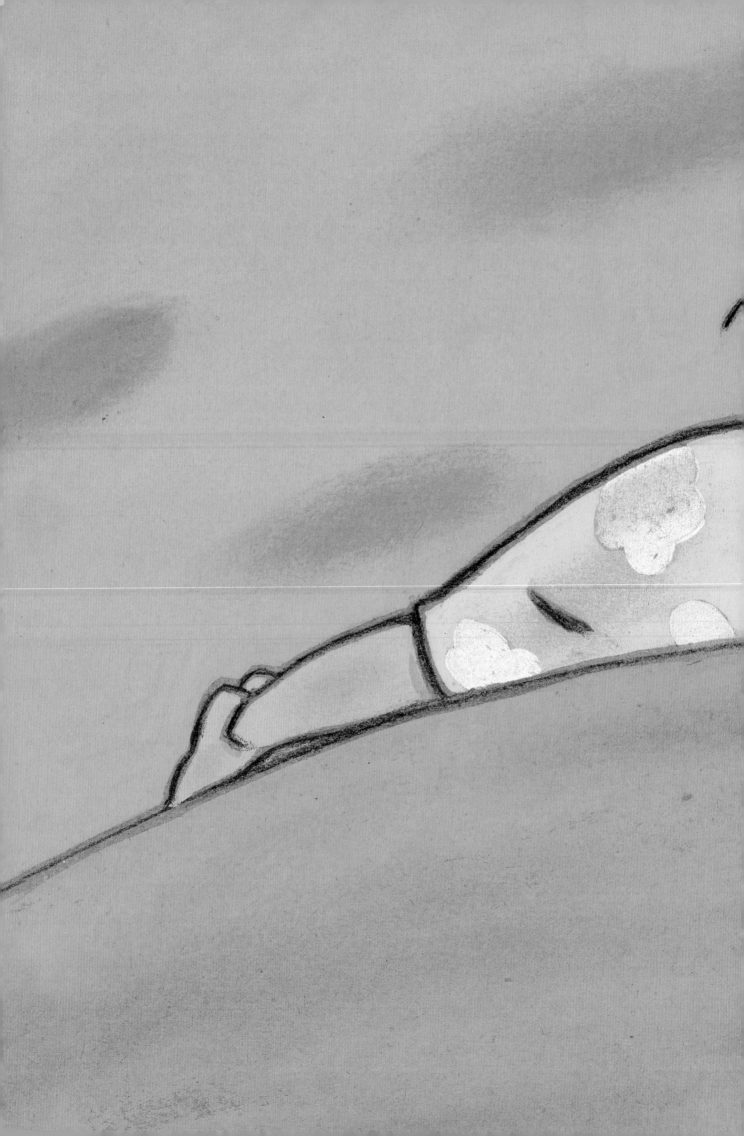

My mummy's favourite dress
is blue with little clouds on it.
When she wears it, the sky
is never grey.

When my mummy plants seeds, flowers always grow. Sometimes they grow even taller than me! That's magic.

Butterflies come and listen
when my mummy sings.
That's magic.

But sometimes *I'm* the magic one.
When I sing and dance,
my mummy always laughs.

I love it when my mummy
makes cakes. For my birthday
she made the biggest cake ever.
It was as big as a rocket!

When my mummy tells
me stories, my bed turns
into a ship and we go on
an adventure together.
That's magic.

But when my mummy
tells me she loves me . . .

that's the most magic
thing of all.